First published in the United States, Great Britain, Canada,
Australia, and New Zealand in 2001 by North-South Books,
an imprint of Nord-Süd Verlag AG, Gossau Zürich, Switzerland.

Distributed in the United States by North-South Books Inc., New York.

Library of Congress Cataloging-in-Publication Data is available.
A CIP catalogue record for this book is available from The British Library.
ISBN 0-7358-1507-0 (trade binding) 10 9 8 7 6 5 4 3 2 1
ISBN 0-7358-1508-9 (library binding) 10 9 8 7 6 5 4 3 2 1
Printed in Italy

For more information about our books, and the authors and artists
who create them, visit our web site: www.northsouth.com

Translated by J. Alison James

A Michael Neugebauer Book
North-South Books / New York / London

Raoul Krischanitz

molto's dream

Molto was a big tiger cat who had better toys than anyone around. But he was not happy. He had a wish that couldn't be granted. He wanted to see the world from above. Often he turned his back on the pile of toys and climbed up to the crook of the old linden tree. There he would dream that he could fly like a bird.

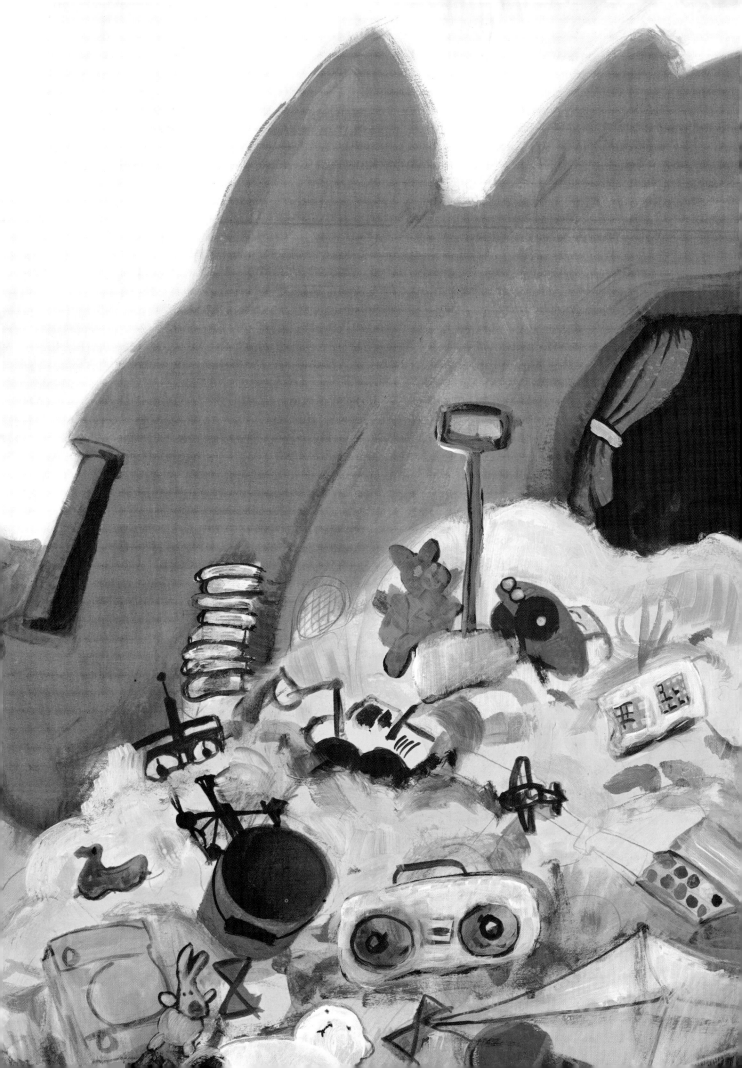

One morning Molto caught two kittens playing with one of his balls.
"That's mine!" snarled Molto. "Leave it alone!"

"But you have lots of other balls!" said Luna.
"You can play with us, too," said Felix.
"I don't want to play!" whined Molto. "And
  I don't want to share."

"What *do* you want then?" asked Luna.

Molto sighed. "What I really want is to fly," he said quietly. "I long to see the world from above."

"Well," Luna said. "What if we lift you up?"

"No, that wouldn't be high enough," said Molto.

"You could climb a tree," said Felix.

"I've done that. It's not high enough either."

"Or go to the top of Round Mountain," suggested Luna.

"Still not enough."

"Then you'll have to turn into a bird," cried Felix.

"He can't do that," Luna said. "A cat can only be a cat."

Molto looked so sad that Felix felt sorry for him. "We'll think of something," promised Felix.

The kittens said good-bye. But the next morning they were back, and they brought a thick book.

"Look what we've found, Molto!" they cried excitedly. "If you can't fly yourself, you need something to fly in. An airplane is too hard, but we might be able to build a balloon!"

This was it! This was the idea they were looking for. Quickly they set to work.

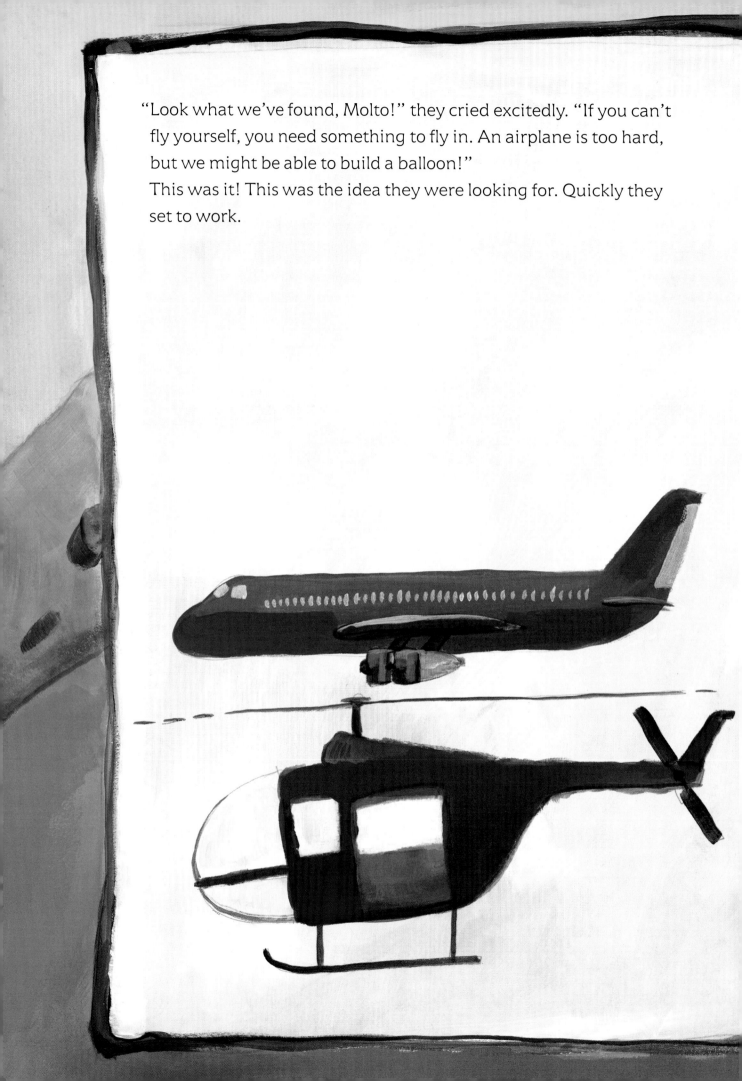

Day after day they rummaged and tinkered, pondered and pounded. As they worked, they talked about what it would be like to see the world from above. And then one day, there it was: their amazing hot-air balloon!

"Hurrah! I can fly at last!" cried Molto. Without a thought, he bounded into the basket and cast off the line.

"What about us?" cried Luna and Felix, but Molto didn't listen.

The balloon rose into the air high above the clouds.

Shaking their heads, Felix and Luna watched him go.

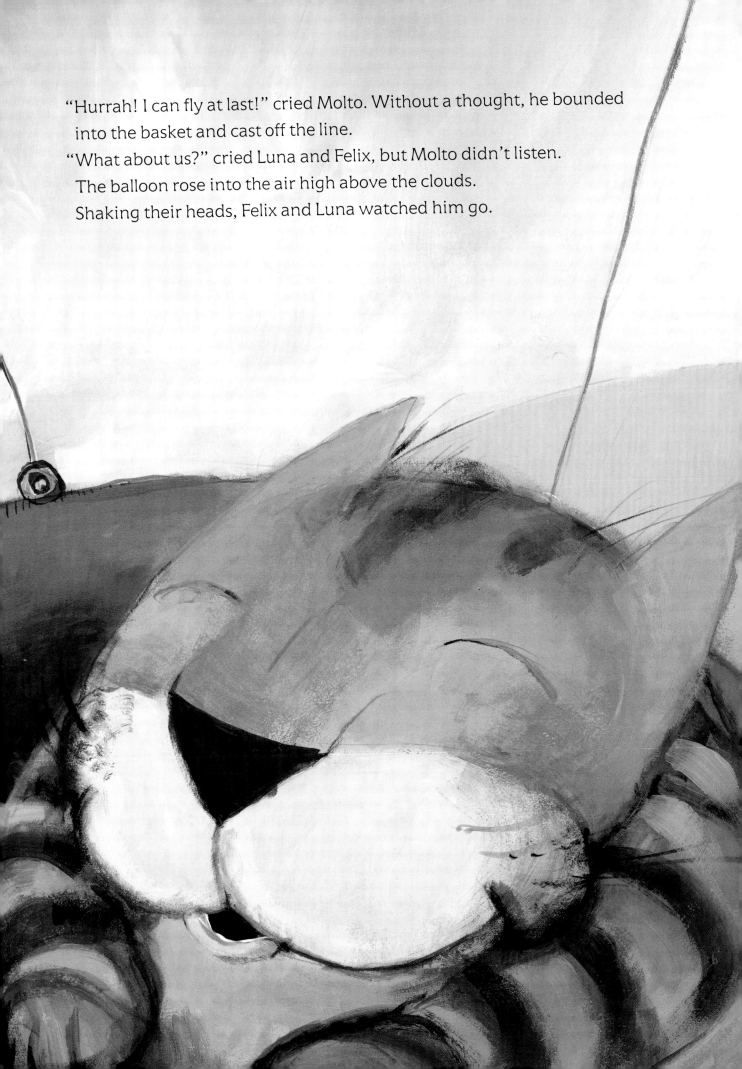

At first Molto was thrilled when he looked down at the world below. He was flying! Really flying! Molto saw his house, the linden tree, Round Mountain. How lovely it all looked. But something was missing. Molto saw Felix and Luna playing together in the meadow. They were running and rolling in the grass. They seemed to have forgotten Molto and his balloon.

Molto suddenly felt lonely. He remembered Luna saying she wanted to see what sheep looked like from high in the air. Felix said he wanted to see the boats. Now Molto could see everything, but they weren't here to share it. He would just have to take them up tomorrow, he decided.

But it was windy when he landed. The balloon twisted and ripped on the fence. It would never fly again. Felix and Luna weren't there to see the wreck. They didn't visit Molto that night or the next night, either. Molto felt terrible. He knew why they stayed away. He could think of only one thing to do.

One morning Molto came to find Felix and Luna.
"Hello, you two!" he greeted them cheerfully. "I have a surprise for you.
Won't you come and see?"

"What kind of surprise?" whispered Felix to Luna. "A new toy that he won't let us play with?"
But no, it was better than a toy, and it was made to share. . . .

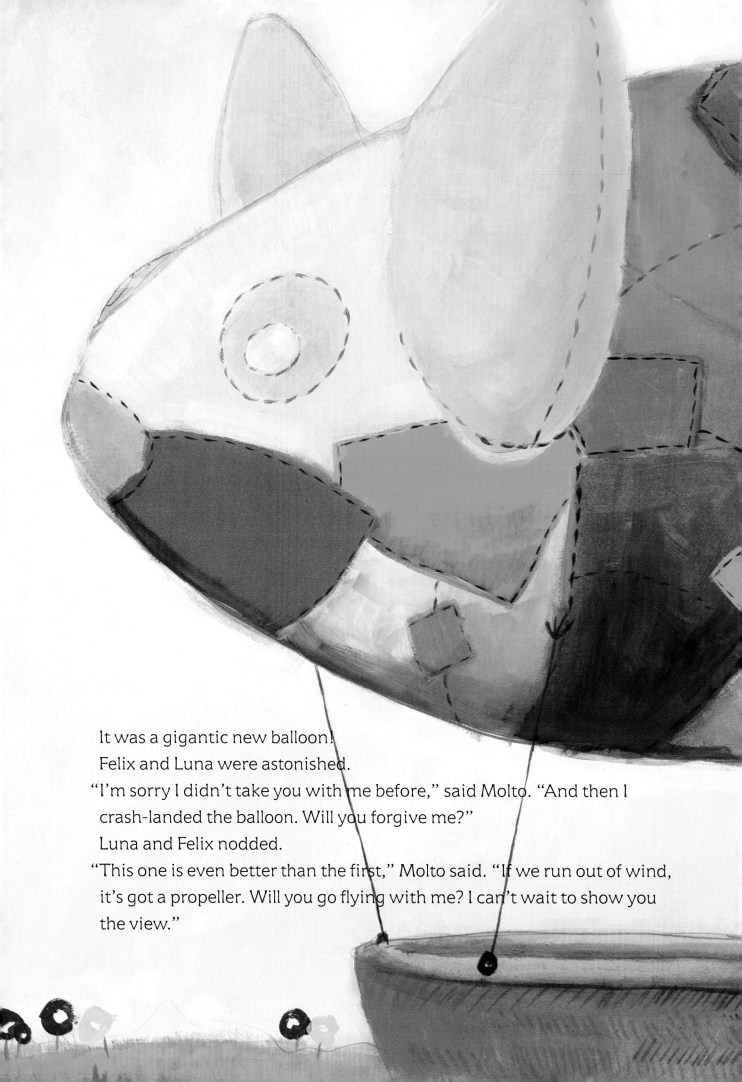

It was a gigantic new balloon!
Felix and Luna were astonished.
"I'm sorry I didn't take you with me before," said Molto. "And then I
    crash-landed the balloon. Will you forgive me?"
Luna and Felix nodded.
"This one is even better than the first," Molto said. "If we run out of wind,
    it's got a propeller. Will you go flying with me? I can't wait to show you
    the view."

Molto untied the lines and off they flew.
The balloon rose above the old linden, above Round Mountain, even above the clouds. They were higher than Molto, Felix, and Luna had ever dreamed possible.
"Oh wow, meow!" cried Luna and Felix, excited. "Flying is wonderful!"

"Yes," agreed Molto, a big smile lighting up his face. "And it's even better when you share it with your friends."